To my hero, my daddy, Clebe McClary.

And to my she-ro, my mother, Deanna.

"Love is not self seeking," says 1 Corinthians 13:5.

I am reminded of that truth every time I think of you.

To learn more about the real-life couple featured in this book, check out *Commitment to Love* by Deanna McClary and Jerry B. Jenkins (Nashville: Thomas Nelson, 1989).

isyourdadapirate.com

www.mascotbooks.com

Is Your Dad a Pirate?

For more information, please contact:
Mascot Books
560 Herndon Parkway #120
Herndon, VA 20170
info@mascotbooks.com

Library of Congress Control Number: 2017907153

CPSIA Code: PRT0617A
ISBN-13: 978-1-68401-319-7

Printed in the United States

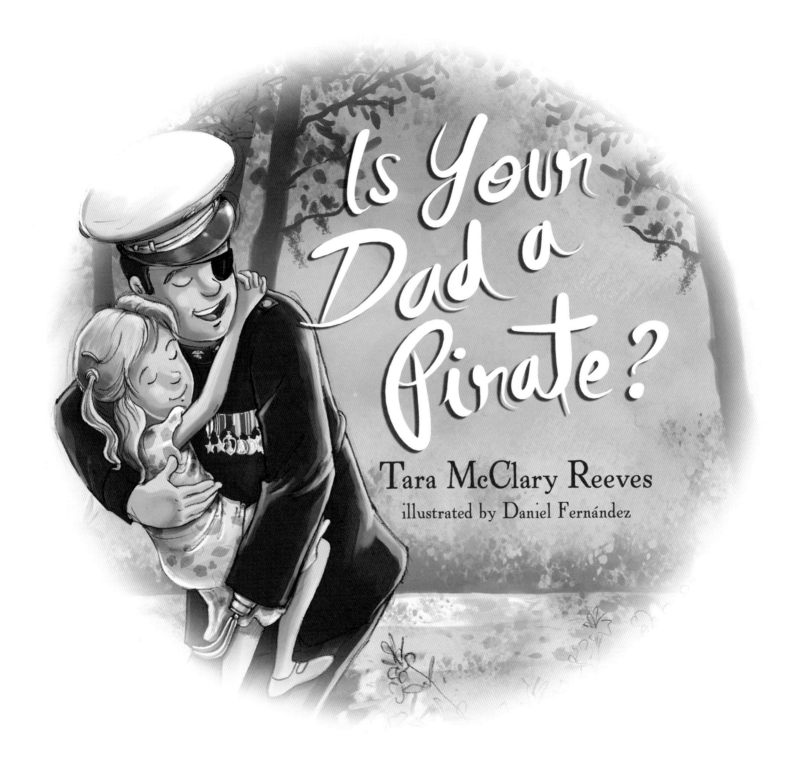

Is Your Dad a Pirate?

Tara McClary Reeves

illustrated by Daniel Fernández

When my daddy went away to fight for our country, I worried.

Mommy and I prayed for
him every night.

It made me happy when he'd call.

Each week we wrote to Daddy. I'd always enclose a picture of what I imagined us doing together when he returned home.

I colored us fishing in my grandpa's pond. I painted us jumping waves at the ocean. I drew us throwing the football.

One afternoon, our family got a call that made Mommy cry.

I cried, too, when Mommy said Daddy would look different in future pictures I'd create.

But I loved my daddy no matter what he looked like on the outside. I was just happy God brought him back to us.

I colored us reeling in a big trout. I painted us splashing in the ocean. I drew us running for a touchdown.

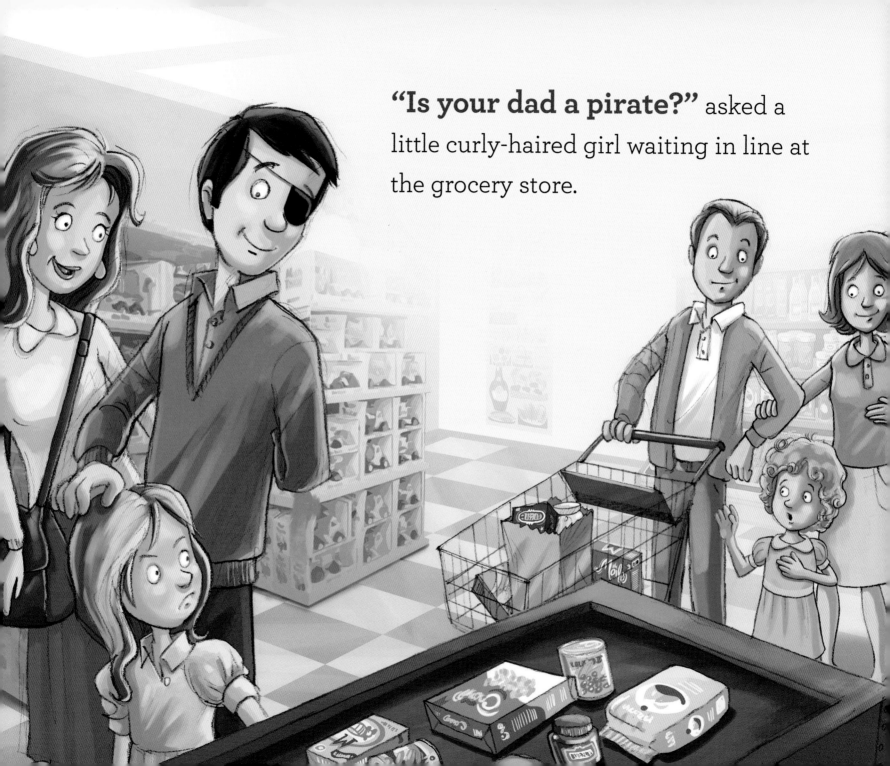

"Is your dad a pirate?" asked a little curly-haired girl waiting in line at the grocery store.

I felt my face getting hot.
I get that question a lot.

Daddy smiled. He let the girl look under his sleeve and touch the black patch over his left eye.

"How'd you lose your eye and arm?" Miss Goldilocks wanted to know.

Mommy overheard.

"Oh, sweetheart," she explained, "my husband didn't lose his eye or his arm. He gave them in service to our country."

Mommy always has a great way
of explaining everything.

People get to learn about the kind of sacrifice my daddy made when they watch the news, but many don't know about my mommy's. I do.

In the morning,
Mommy buttons
Daddy's shirt for him.

She buckles his belt.
And she ties his shoes.

Daddy gives her little
love taps along the way.

Yesterday, on the playground,
some kids ran over to us.
"Is your dad a pirate?"
one asked.

It was me who smiled and
spoke this time.

"No," I answered.

"He's a veteran, **a hero**."

"And he married one, too."